MONEY AND FINANCIAL INSTITUTIONS

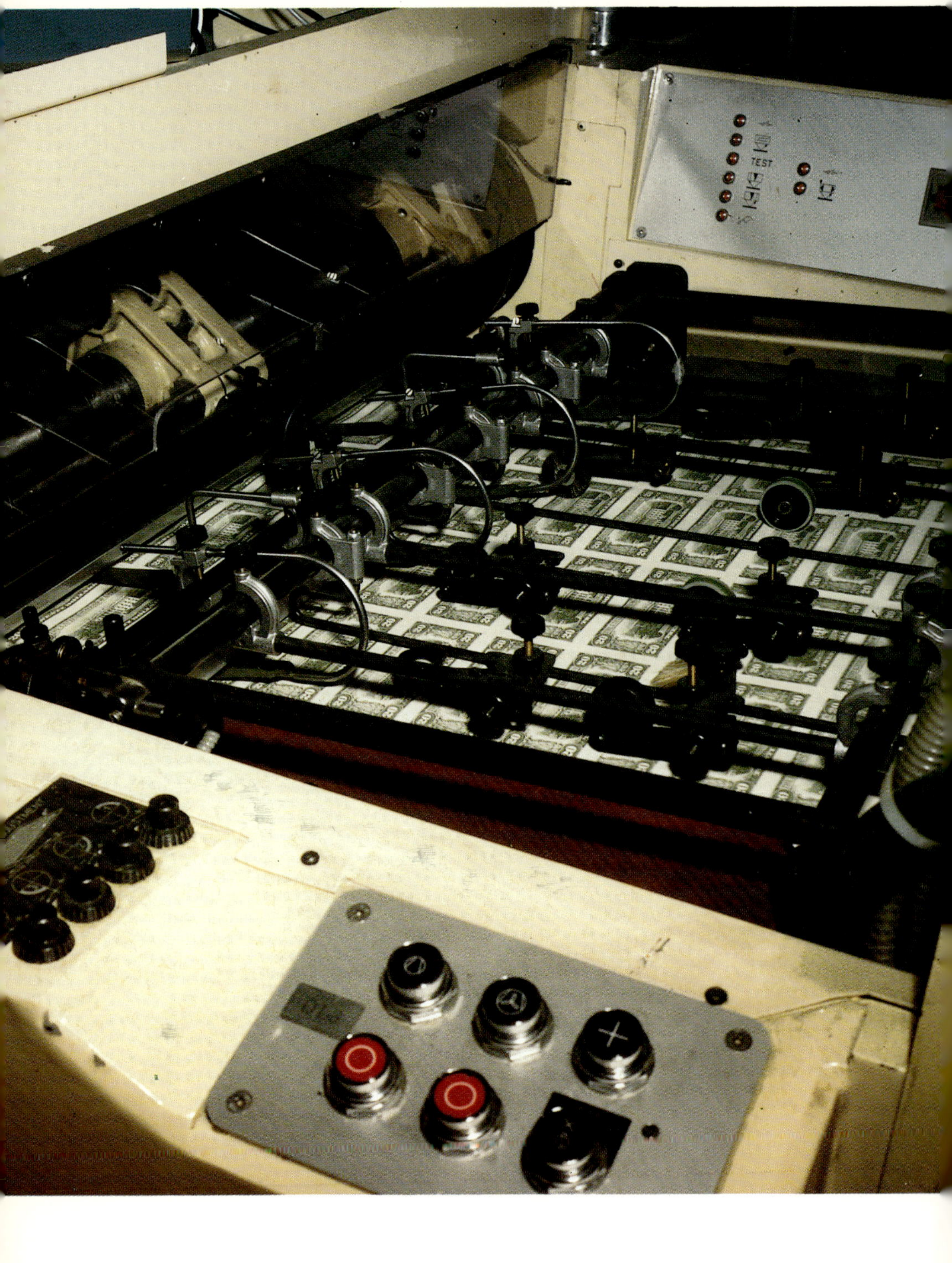
TEST

ECONOMICS FOR TODAY

MONEY AND FINANCIAL INSTITUTIONS

Jane E. Bungum

Series Editor: M. Barbara Killen
Professor, University of Minnesota

Lerner Publications Company ▪ Minneapolis, Minnesota

The photograph on page 2 shows money being printed at the Bureau of Engraving and Printing.

Words that appear in **bold** type are listed in a glossary that starts on page 90.

Library of Congress Cataloging-in-Publication Data

Bungum, Jane E.
Economics for today : money and financial institutions / Jane E. Bungum.
p. cm.—(Economics for today)
Includes bibliographical references and index.
Summary: Studies the concepts and forms of money and banking, purchasing power, saving, spending, and borrowing, and examines the operation of institutions that facilitate financial transactions.
ISBN 0-8225-1781-7 (lib. bdg.)
1. Money—United States—Juvenile literature. 2. Financial institutions—United States—Juvenile literature. 3. Monetary policy—United States—Juvenile literature. [1. Money. 2. Financial institutions.] I. Title. II. Series.

HG540.B86 1991
332.1—dc20

90-41649
CIP
AC

Manufactured in the United States of America

1 2 3 4 5 6 7 8 9 10 00 99 98 97 96 95 94 93 92 91

CONTENTS

1

MONEY—FROM YAP TO BLIP

What do you think of when you hear the word *money*? Do you think of how much you have—or don't have? Do you think of what you want to buy next and how long it will take to save enough to make that purchase? Maybe you plan ways to earn money.

It's amazing that simple pieces of metal and paper mean so much to people. But that's part of the intrigue of money. We are not fascinated by the pieces of paper and metal themselves so much as what they can offer us. In addition to the basic necessities of food, clothing, and shelter, money allows us to listen to our favorite music, ride a new bike, or see the latest movie.

It's hard to imagine life without money. The beds we sleep in cost money. We have to pay for the food we eat, the clothes we wear, and the gas we put in our cars. No wonder people sometimes seem obsessed with money!

People who lived thousands of years ago understood the value of trade. They didn't use paper and metal money, but they knew the value of an animal hide. Besides being useful as protection against the cold, an animal hide could be traded for more food or better tools.

Forms of Money

Money can be any object that people agree to use as a form of payment for goods and services. (Services cannot be stored; they are usually used right away, such as a haircut or a meal in a restaurant.) For an object to have value as money, people must accept it as a **medium of exchange**, or form of payment.

Throughout history, people have used a variety of objects to pay for goods and services. Money has taken many forms, depending on the needs of a community and the resources available at the time. Whale teeth, shells, beads, chocolate, tea, rice, cigarettes, marbles, spices, and even wrapped candies have all been used as money.

One of the most unique forms of money ever used was exchanged in the Pacific island country of Yap. During the 1800s, the citizens of Yap used huge stone coins called *Fe.* (The term "pocket change" takes on a whole new meaning!) Although Fe was accepted by the citizens of Yap, in most modern societies giant stones

Lydian coins were made of lumps of metal stamped with a design.

would not be practical as a medium of exchange, since they would be so difficult to carry around.

Early Coin and Currency

In the United States, the two most common forms of money are coin money and paper money. Coin money is known as **specie**. Paper money is referred to as **currency**. (Coin and paper money are both also called *cash.*) Both forms have been around for centuries.

Some of the oldest coins were made around 600 B.C. in Lydia, an ancient country that is now part of western Turkey. Lydian coins were bean-shaped, made of a mixture of gold and silver, and stamped with a design. People in ancient China used bronze coins molded in the shape of cattle and hides as early as 1300 B.C. Historians have

In Europe during the Middle Ages, many people raised their own food and animals, such as cows that provided milk.

found evidence of bronze coin money used in Egypt and Babylon during the eighth century B.C. The Chinese also used the first paper money.

As trade expanded among nations and conquering armies brought coin and paper money back to their homelands, the use of currency and coin spread throughout Asia and Europe.

Money in the Middle Ages

In Europe during the Middle Ages—the period from about A.D. 500 to 1500—most families were self-sufficient. They built their own homes, raised their own food, and made their own clothes. They had little need for paper or coin money. Coin money was available, but it was used mainly by merchants and rulers. Most people got what they could not produce on their own through **barter**—the direct exchange of goods for other goods. Individuals traded the goods they produced for goods produced by others. Barter was the easiest and most common way to exchange goods.

A barter system works well if both trading partners make something that the other person wants and needs, and the two can agree on a fair trade. For instance, a farmer may trade a shoemaker five bushels of corn for a new pair of shoes. But what happens if the shoemaker doesn't want corn? Bartering can be time-consuming and cumbersome.

As trading activity increased, the need for a more efficient way to exchange goods grew. Certain items began to be identified as particularly valuable as a means of payment. Agricultural products such as cattle, corn, rice, and wheat were used as money. These types of payments are known as **commodity money**. Commodity money is still used in some countries.

Money and the Industrial Revolution

During the 1700s, cities such as London grew into large centers of trade. Factories were built, and goods that were once produced by individual craftsmen began to be mass-produced. These developments, part of the Industrial Revolution, changed the way people worked. Jobs became specialized; workers made only one small part of an item, rather than the whole product. Citizens moved from rural areas to cities, drawn by the promise of jobs and a better life.

In an urban and industrial society, barter was no longer practical. What did factory workers have to barter with when they went to buy food at the market? People no longer grew their own food and sewed their own clothing. They needed a commonly accepted form of payment to buy goods and services.

Governments responded by issuing more money made of metal and paper. They **minted**, or made, coin money stamped with images of the king or ruler. People began using coin and currency more than barter or commodity money. Even though currency and coins were much easier to transport than other forms of money (cattle, for instance, could die on the way to market), people risked being robbed when they carried money.

A traveler is robbed of his sack of money in this detail from a picture printed in the Middle Ages.

Goldsmiths—people who minted coins—began to store and guard money for customers. The goldsmiths would write a letter that stated the amount of money someone had in storage. People could use these letters to buy goods, so they didn't have to carry large amounts of money around with them. These notes became known as **letters of credit**. The goldsmith would then pay the seller the amount that was due.

Function over Form

No matter what form money takes—whether it's giant stones or whale teeth—one feature always remains the same. The object's value is not in its form but in its function. The most important thing is that the object is accepted as a means of payment.

When the people of Lydia first began minting coins, they used gold or silver. Gold and silver are limited natural resources. These precious metals are considered valuable in and of themselves. The worth of each coin was based on the amount of gold or silver in it. Money was said to be **gold-** or **silver-backed**—currency or coin that could be exchanged for gold or silver.

But as trading among people in different parts of the world expanded, Lydia and other countries began to experience gold and silver shortages.There was just not enough gold and silver in every country. Without enough gold and silver to use for money, it was hard to continue trading. Countries that didn't have natural supplies of gold and silver were "cash poor." It was difficult for them to trade. Finally, people began hoarding gold and silver, making trade nearly impossible.

In the late 1700s, the Scottish economist Adam Smith wrote, "Money makes goods move." He said that no matter what form money takes—whether it is made of a precious metal or of paper—its worth was in its ability to serve as a medium of exchange. Smith said that the real value of money is to help goods move quickly and easily between buyers and sellers.

Money that doesn't have value in and of itself, such as paper money, is referred to as **fiat money**. The value of fiat money comes from the fact that it is accepted by the people using it and the government issuing it. People have to trust that the money has value. Most countries now use fiat money.

A Common Form of Payment

In order for a money system to work, people first have to agree on the actual object to be used—whether that is whale teeth, giant stone coins, or paper.

Second, everyone must have confidence in the money; they must believe that it will hold its value over time and that it is not **counterfeit**—or fake. If people are not confident in the medium of exchange, they will find another form of payment.

Finally, the form that money takes must be **liquid**—that is, it must be able to be converted quickly and easily into a commonly accepted form of payment. For example, a person could trade a piece of land for goods and services, but the land might not always be accepted by the seller. It takes time to sell land to get a more common medium of exchange, cash. Not only does the sales process take time, but the price of the land could change.

Land is not considered liquid in the way cash is.

Money at the Speed of Light

Money continues to appear in a variety of forms that represent changing needs and values. During World War II, prisoners of war used cigarettes as a form of payment. Wrapped hard candies are used to make small change in some southern European countries. Commodity money is still used in some countries. Credit cards, nicknamed "plastic" money, are common.

Computers now move money around the world at the speed of light. Bank computers can be programmed to electronically move funds from one bank account into another. No money physically changes hands. Amounts of money are seen as blips on a computer screen.

A common form of electronic payment is direct deposit of paychecks. An employer can deposit, or place, an employee's salary directly into the person's checking or savings account. Employees do not have to worry about paychecks being lost or stolen. They are assured of having funds immediately available on payday, and they don't even have to go to the bank to deposit their paychecks.

MORE ABOUT MONEY

What is the purpose of money? It seems like a simple question. Usually we only notice the results of money—new clothes, a place to live, food to eat. What makes it possible for pieces of paper and metal to provide us with these basic needs? Money has four basic functions.

Accepted Medium of Exchange

First, money must be accepted by a wide variety of people. Suppose that blue jeans are the accepted medium of exchange in

2

the country where you live. You want to buy a new bike that costs 25 pairs of jeans. On a sunny Saturday morning, you pack up your "money" and go down to the bike shop. The shop manager examines all 25 pairs of jeans and then informs you that 5 pairs are not acceptable because they have holes in the knees.

"They simply aren't fit," says the manager. "Come back when you have five more acceptable pairs of jeans."

"Wait a minute!" you protest. "The jeans with holes in the knees are great. Kids love them."

"I don't care," the store owner replies. "You'll have to bring me five more pairs with no holes or I won't sell you the bike."

Disappointed, you leave the bike shop. "All I want to do is buy a bike," you think to yourself. "I don't want to spend all of my time trying to find jeans that are accepted by the bike shop."

Imagine the same situation on a larger scale. Every time you wanted to buy something, you would have to spend time negotiating with the buyer about whether or not your jeans were acceptable as payment. If you used currency and coin, however, the store owner would accept your money even if it looked worn or torn. The money would still represent its agreed-upon value.

Standard Measure of Value

A second purpose of money is to act as a standard measure of value. To the store owner, the jeans with the holes in the knees were of less value than the ones without holes. Not all pairs of jeans were seen as having the same value.

Money must function as a common yardstick to measure value. Whether you use four quarters, ten dimes, or a one-dollar bill, they all represent one dollar's worth of purchasing power. And every one-dollar bill is equally valuable.

Store of Value

Money needs to function as a **store of value**. That means that money should hold its power to purchase the same amount of goods and services over time. If you decide to save money for a future purchase, you want to feel confident that your money will still be able to buy just as much at a later date as it could today. When money doesn't hold its value over time, people lose confidence in it.

Money is not the only store of value, or wealth. Other items that hold value over time include gold, jewels, real estate, and paintings.

Standard of Deferred Payment

One problem that people encounter when using commodity money as a form of payment is that the commodity can spoil or, as with cattle, the money could die! Money must be able to stand up to the test of time. It must act as a standard of deferred—or later—payment.

Inflation affects the value of money. Inflation is a continual rise in the price of goods and services. As prices rise, the value of money declines, because its purchasing power goes down. For example, in 1980 a candy bar cost 30 cents. Ten years later, it cost 45 cents.

Common Characteristics of Money

The money used around the world comes in many colors, shapes, and sizes. Yet it has several common characteristics. It is convenient, durable, and divisible.

Unlike the large stone coins used on Yap, U.S. money can be carried conveniently in a purse or pocket. A $50 bill weighs no more than a $5 bill. A $100 check isn't any more difficult or costly to mail than a $1 check.

Coin money is very durable. Coins can be in circulation for years and not wear out. The life span of currency isn't as long as that of coins, but the special paper used in currency is designed to withstand high use. The higher the dollar value of the bill, the longer it usually lasts. This is because the higher value bills are not used as frequently by consumers as are ones, fives, and tens. A $1 bill has a life span of 15 to 18 months.

U.S. money is also divisible. That is, it comes in a variety of forms—from 1-cent coins to $100 notes—so that we can easily pay for goods that cost only a few pennies or hundreds of dollars. The different dollar amounts are referred to as the bill's **denomination**.

How Money Is Made

The Department of the Treasury, an arm of the U.S. government, is responsible for making currency and coin. U.S. currency is printed in Washington, D.C., by the Bureau of Engraving and Printing. Highly skilled engravers cut the features of a bill—which is called a **Federal Reserve note**—into a steel plate. Each feature of a note, such as the portrait, lettering, and scrollwork, is engraved separately. No one person is trained to engrave all parts

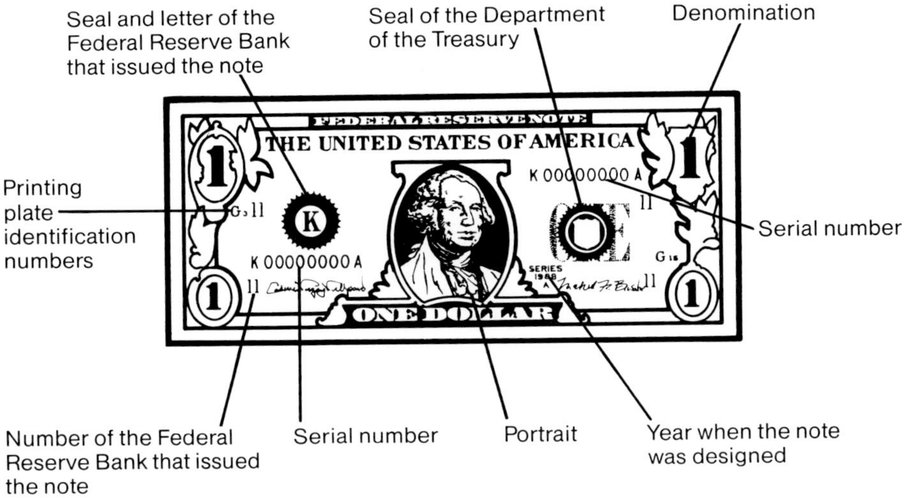

Features of a Federal Reserve note

of a note. This prevents anyone from learning how to engrave a fake bill. The intricate scrollwork on U.S. currency is created by a machine. The currency is printed on high-quality, sturdy paper. Secret formula inks are used to print the currency.

Coins are made—or minted—by the U.S. Mint under the direction of the treasury. Three mints operate in the U.S. The Philadelphia Mint has been in use since 1792. The Denver Mint began making coins in 1906. The San Francisco Mint closed in 1955 and reopened in 1965.

To make coins, strips of metal are rolled to the proper thickness of the coin being produced, the way you would roll out dough to make cut-out cookies. Blank coins are then punched from the strips of metal. After the blank coins are heated and cleaned, they are stamped with a design on the front and back.

At the Bureau of Engraving and Printing, money is printed in large sheets and cut into individual notes.

The treasury delivers currency and coin in unmarked trucks to each of the 12 Federal Reserve banks. The **Federal Reserve** is the central bank of the United States. It serves as a bank for other financial institutions and the U.S. government. Banks, credit unions, and savings and loans order currency and coin from these reserve banks. Customers of financial institutions withdraw coin and currency from their bank accounts as they need them.

There is a constant flow of money between people, financial institutions, and the Federal Reserve. When customers have more cash on hand than they need, they deposit it at their financial institution. In turn, financial institutions keep their extra cash at the Federal Reserve Bank. The Federal Reserve counts all of the cash it receives and replaces worn, torn, or soiled cash with new currency and coin. The old currency is shredded and thrown away. Worn or damaged coins are returned to the U.S. Mint, where they are melted and reused to make new coins.

Checks, Credit Cards, and Debit Cards

Currency and coin are much more convenient than commodity money, but even cash can be cumbersome. One million dollars in $1 bills weighs over 40 pounds. While most people don't buy things that cost $1 million, carrying or mailing large sums of cash can be difficult and unsafe. Other forms of money, such as checks, can be more convenient than cash.

The origin of checking accounts may be in the Middle Ages, when goldsmiths began to offer safekeeping services for people who did not want to carry large sums of money. **Checks** are written instructions to take money from the financial institution account of the person

Old or worn currency is shredded at the Federal Reserve.

Checks allow people to pay large amounts of money with a single piece of paper. Most people pay bills with checks, because they are easy to send through the mail.

writing the check. Checks are convenient and safe. They allow people to exchange large amounts of money with a single piece of paper. Only the individual or company whose name is written on the check is supposed to "cash" the check—exchange it for cash at a bank—or deposit it in a bank.

Credit cards are an easy way to pay for goods and services. But credit cards are not money in the real sense of the word. When you use **credit** to make a purchase, you are borrowing money you don't have.

Financial institutions and credit card companies give credit cards to people who can repay purchases "charged" against their credit card accounts. Merchants put a credit card through a machine that records the card's information on a sales receipt. Copies of the receipt go to the merchant, the customer, and the credit card company. The credit card company pays the merchant and bills the credit cardholder for the amount of goods charged.

People like to use credit cards because the cards allow them to "buy now, pay later." Credit cards are also convenient and accepted throughout the world. For the use of the credit card privilege, the company usually charges the cardholder a fee.

Debit cards offer consumers a checkless, cashless way to make purchases. Debit cards are sort of like electronic checks. Rather than writing a check, consumers use a plastic card to pay for goods and services. But it isn't a credit card. With a debit card, money is transferred electronically from the customer's checking account to the debit card company, which in turn pays the merchant. Not all stores accept debit cards.

Fake Money

Printing currency and minting coins are not easy processes. They are not meant to be! The intricate printing process and the special materials used to produce currency and coin help prevent people from illegally making their own counterfeit money. Government officials go to great lengths to mint coins and print currency that is difficult to reproduce.

How do you spot a counterfeit note? One way to spot a fake is to study the real thing. Genuine currency is printed on very high-quality paper with red and blue threads in it. Counterfeit currency may look and feel different, because the red and blue "threads" may just be drawn or printed. Genuine currency has crisp, unbroken lines in the portrait and scrollwork. The serial numbers on the notes are evenly printed and well spaced.

Law enforcement officials and the United States Secret Service investigate counterfeit money schemes. People who are convicted of making counterfeit money can be fined up to $5,000 or put in jail for up to 15 years.

3

THE POWER TO PURCHASE

Money gives us the ability—or power—to purchase the goods and services we want. Most of us exchange our time and effort—in other words, we work—to produce a product or provide a service. In return, we receive money, often in the form of a paycheck. Then we each decide how to spend our money.

Spending

While everybody's needs and desires are different, Americans as a whole spend money in similar ways. In the U.S., people spend

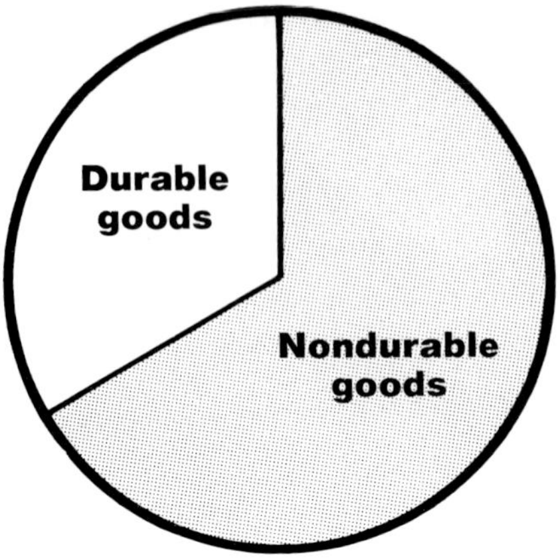

As the pie chart at the left shows, people in the U.S. spend about one-third of their money on durable goods, such as cars, and two-thirds on nondurable goods, such as food. The graph below shows the spending habits of people in the U.S., Germany, and Japan.

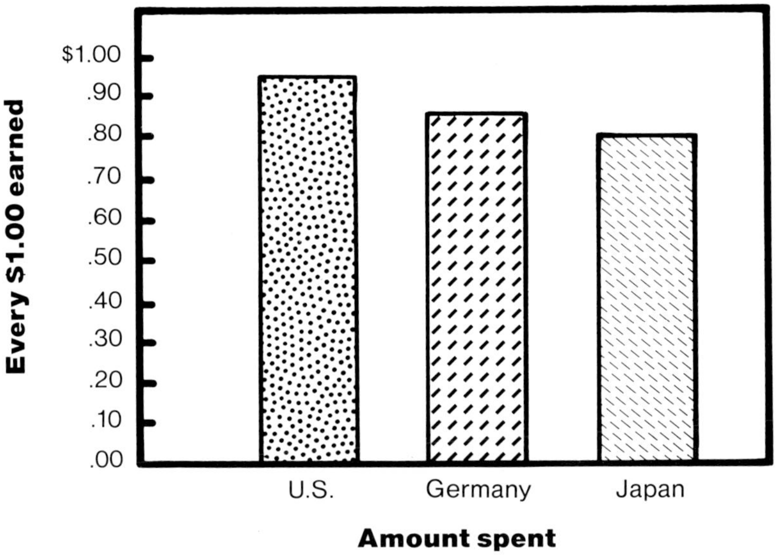

about two-thirds of their money on **nondurable goods** (items that are used each day, like food and clothing) and services (like meals in restaurants and dry cleaning).

The remainder of the money is spent on **durable goods** —items that last a long time, such as television sets, washing machines, and cars.

U.S. citizens' spending habits aren't the same as those of people in other countries. Americans spend about 95 percent of what they earn, or 95 cents out of every dollar. Germans spend less, about 85 cents for every dollar earned. The Japanese spend only 80 percent of what they earn.

Borrowing

Some purchases cost so much that we must borrow money to pay for them. For example, most people borrow money to buy a car or a house. By borrowing money, we give up some of our future purchasing power. We commit money that we will earn in the future to pay for goods we use now. Here's an example of how borrowing works.

Sam and Chris Jackson are excited about the new baby on the way. But they don't know where they're going to put it! With two other children, Sam and Chris are just about out of space in their home. Rather than buy another house, the Jacksons have decided to build an addition onto their home. To do that, they'll need to borrow money. They've set up an appointment with Ellen Strauss, an officer at Second National Bank, to discuss getting a **loan**.

"Congratulations, Mr. and Mrs. Jackson," says Ms. Strauss. "It's always exciting when a baby is on the way."

"We'd like to add another bedroom and a second bathroom to our house," explains Chris. "We've had the plans drawn up and have gotten estimates on what it would cost to do the work. Now all we need is the money to get going!"

Ellen reviews the cost estimates for the addition and then explains what the bank will take into consideration in granting a loan. First the bank looks at the borrower's work and credit history, or how reliable the person has been in keeping a job and paying bills. While it isn't always necessary, the bank likes to see that the applicant has worked at the same job and lived in the same place for at least two years.

The bank also wants to make certain that the Jacksons have enough money to repay the loan. The loan application that they'll fill out asks questions about how much money they earn, their monthly expenses—including other loan payments—and the number of people they support.

Finally, the bank asks about the borrower's **collateral**—does the couple own anything that the bank could sell, such as an automobile, if neither of them can pay back the loan?

"So where do we start?" asks Sam.

"Start by filling out the loan application," says Ellen. "When you've completed it, the bank will check to make sure that the information you've given us is correct."

"We would like to get started on this addition as soon as possible," says Chris. "How long will it take to find out whether or not Second National will lend us the money?"

"We are required by law to approve or deny the loan in writing within 30 days," says Ellen.

"Great," exclaims Sam. "We'll have enough time to finish the addition before the new addition arrives!"

Most people must borrow money to buy a new house.

APPLICATION PLEASE PRINT OR TYPE

DATE	SOCIAL SECURITY NUMBER	DRIVERS LICENSE	ACCOUNT NUMBER

You/We apply for credit under the terms disclosed in the Credit Agreement and Truth-in-Lending Disclosure.

You REQUEST AN ADVANCE of $__________ FOR THE FOLLOWING PURPOSE

Payroll Deduction ☐ Yes ☐ No

CREDIT INSURANCE STATEMENT OF INTENT

Check if Coverage is Desired: ☐ CREDIT DISABILITY ☐ SINGLE CREDIT LIFE ☐ JOINT CREDIT LIFE

The credit union will disclose the cost of this voluntary insurance to you. A separate insurance election which discloses the terms and conditions of the credit insurance must be signed in order for the coverage to become effective. We will mail this to you.

Print full name (including full middle name)	Date of birth	Name of co-applicant / Co-applicant's social security number		Number of dependents including yourself	Phone number with area code
Home address	City	County	State	Zip code	How long there?
Previous address, city, state					How long there?
Your present employer or source of income	Address			Phone	How long
Your occupation	Department				Gross income
Previous employer	Address				How long?
Co-applicant's employer or source of income	Address			How long	Gross income
Other income - source *(Note: Income from alimony, child support, or maintenance income need not be shown here unless you will rely upon it as a basis for undertaking or repaying this loan.)*					Amount *(week, month)* $ Per
Name of nearest relative not living with me		Address			Phone
Name of co-applicant's nearest relative		Address			Phone

Financial Statement

*This Statement may be completed jointly by both married and unmarried co-borrowers if their assets and liabilities are sufficiently joined; Otherwise separate statements are required.

ASSETS / **LIABILITIES AND NET WORTH**

Description	Cash or market value	Installment debts (include "revolving charge accts")	Delinquent amount	Balance	Monthly payments
Savings accounts	$			$	$
Checking accounts					
Stocks and bonds					
Life insurance net cash value *Face amount ($*					
SUBTOTAL LIQUID ASSETS	$	Day care			
Real estate owned *(enter market value)*		Mortgage payments or rent			
Vested interest in retirement fund					
Net worth of business owned (ATTACH FINANCIAL STATEMENT)					
Automobiles (make and year)		Automobile loans			
Furniture and personal property		Alimony, child support and maintenance Payments owed to			
Other assets (itemize)		TOTAL MONTHLY PAYMENTS		$	$

*This Statement may be completed jointly by both married and unmarried co-borrowers if their assets and liabilities are sufficiently joined; Otherwise separate statements are required.

Everything that you have stated in this application is correct to the best of your knowledge. The Credit Union is authorized to check your credit, employment history, obtain a credit report and to answer questions about their credit experience with you. You understand that it may be a federal crime punishable by fine or imprisonment, or both, to knowingly make any false statements concerning any of the above facts as applicable under the provisions of the United States Criminal Code.

APPLICANT'S SIGNATURE	DATE	CO-APPLICANT'S SIGNATURE	DATE
X SEAL		X SEAL	

This loan application from a credit union requires borrowers to answer several questions about their earnings and debts.

Interest

Borrowing money comes with a price. We must follow the rules of the financial institution that loans us the money. Those rules—or terms—determine when the loan must be paid back and the amount of each payment we have to make.

Typically, financial institutions require that a loan be repaid in monthly **installments** (small portions of the money borrowed). The original loan amount is called the **principal**. In addition, there is a specific cost for borrowing money. That cost is known as **interest**. Interest is the fee you pay for the privilege of using money that you have borrowed. Each month, therefore, the Jacksons will not only have to repay the bank a portion of the money they borrowed for their addition, but they must also pay an additional charge, interest.

The cost of borrowing money is usually stated as an **interest rate**. The interest rate represents a percentage of the loan. For instance, Second National Bank may charge the Jacksons an interest rate of nine percent a year for each dollar they borrow. That means that if the Jacksons were to repay their loan at the end of one year, they would pay back every dollar they borrowed (the principal), plus nine cents per dollar in interest. If their loan was $100, they would repay the $100, plus 9 percent interest, or $9, for a total of $109.

Just as you would shop around for the best price for a pair of new tennis shoes, you should shop around for the best price—or best interest rate—on loans. Financial institutions offer a variety of interest rates on loans. Most people look for an interest rate and terms that they are able to meet.

Saving

You can choose not to spend money on goods and services but to save money instead. People save money for many reasons. One of the most rewarding reasons to save money is for a large purchase, such as a new car, an exotic vacation, or a new home. People also save for future events, such as college or retirement.

Many consumers set money aside for routine payments that are due only a couple times each year, such as tax or insurance payments. By saving a small amount of money each month, people can make these payments when they're due. Saving also gives people the financial security to weather events that no one can plan for, such as major car or home repairs, illness, or unemployment.

By keeping some money set aside in a savings account, people can afford to pay for unexpected expenses, such as car repairs.

Financial institutions offer two basic services—checking and savings accounts—to make spending and saving money convenient. A checking account is an easy, safe way to pay for goods and services without having to carry around large amounts of cash. You can open a checking account by depositing money in a financial institution. In turn, the bank will provide you with checks. When you write a check to make a purchase, the amount of the check is deducted from your account.

Savings accounts are meant to help people save money for future purchases or needs. Financial institutions offer several different types of savings accounts.

Financial institutions pay consumers to save money in checking and savings accounts. The bank pays depositors in the form of interest. In other words, financial institutions pay us for the use of our money. When savers place money in a financial institution, the financial institution uses the money to lend to other consumers and businesses. The borrower pays interest to the bank for the use of this money. In turn, financial institutions use borrowers' interest payments to operate the bank and to pay interest to savers.

Saving money benefits consumers because the money they save earns interest. Saving also benefits the economy as a whole by providing funds to help businesses grow.

4

FINANCIAL INSTITUTIONS: A MARKET FOR MONEY

When you want to buy food, you go to a grocery store. When you want a new outfit, you visit your favorite clothing store. But where do you go if you need money?

Buying and selling money is the business of financial institutions. A financial institution serves as a central meeting place for people with money and people who need money.

History of Banking

As long as there have been two people willing to exchange

goods and services, there has been some form of financial system. The word *bank* comes from the Italian word *banco*, which meant a merchant's bench.

Some of the first people to perform banking functions were the goldsmiths who worked in England and other European countries during the 15th and 16th centuries. Goldsmiths noticed that while they needed to keep a certain amount of gold on hand for when people who had left gold in the goldsmith's safe wanted to take it out, a large amount of gold remained unused.

At the same time, goldsmiths recognized that some people needed to borrow money. They reasoned that since they only needed to keep part of the gold on hand to meet customer demands, the remaining gold could be used for loans. Goldsmiths gave handwritten receipts that borrowers could use as payment for goods or services. In return, borrowers were expected to repay the loan over a certain amount of time, plus pay a service charge in the form of interest. The receipts that the goldsmiths issued added to the amount—or supply—of money in circulation.

This concept of keeping a fraction of gold on reserve and lending the remaining gold was the start of what is called the **fractional reserve system**. Based on the amount of money a financial institution has, it can lend a fraction of its money to consumers and businesses. In doing so, financial institutions help to increase the supply of money in an economy. More money in the economy allows businesses to grow. The fractional reserve system is one of the most important elements in the U.S. banking system.

Soon, goldsmiths' shops became well-known places

Goldsmiths' shops served as early financial institutions.

to make financial transactions. Individuals knew that goldsmiths were willing to lend money. People with extra cash could keep it in a safe place and earn interest.

The meeting places where these early English bankers conducted business did not look much different from modern banks. Customers entered a lobby area where bank workers did business with them over a barred counter, much like modern teller windows.

From the very beginning, goldsmiths—and later financial institutions—found that one of the key elements in providing service to customers was trust. Customers had to trust that the goldsmith wasn't going to run off with their money. Goldsmiths had to rely on the promises that customers made to repay loans.

Banks in Colonial America

In colonial America, people used bills of exchange, barter, and commodity money as payment. (**Bills of exchange** were written agreements that outlined what two trading partners would accept as payment. These bills were sold and resold.) As trading activity increased, colonists found that they needed a more versatile form of money. Settlers from Europe used gold and silver coins brought from their home countries to pay for goods and services. Some colonists used the Native American shell beads called *wampum* as money.

Britain would not allow the colonies to make their own coin money, because the British government wanted to limit the colonies' trading activities. But trade continued to increase in the colonies. Money became scarce. The need for coin got so bad that in 1652, people took matters into their own hands and began secretly minting money in Massachusetts Bay Colony. For the entire 30 years that the mint was in operation, all of the coins were dated 1652, so that the British would not catch on to what the colonists were doing.

The first formal bank in the United States, the Bank of North America, was founded in 1781. The main reason the bank was started was to help the government pay for the expenses of fighting the revolutionary war. Soldiers needed to be fed, clothed, and armed to fight the British. The colonial government recognized the Bank of North

America's notes as **legal tender**—acceptable as money—and used them to pay for the war. After the war was over, in 1783, the bank went out of business.

At the end of the American Revolution, Alexander Hamilton, the country's first secretary of the treasury, convinced Congress that the U.S. needed a strong **central bank**. A central bank could issue a common currency, act as the new government's bank, and ensure that all financial institutions were obeying banking laws. Hamilton had a hard time convincing his fellow politicians, who felt that a central bank would have too much power over money and the economy. Critics worried that a central bank would limit the supply of money. With less money available, trade would slow down.

Finally, in 1791 Congress gave a 21-year **charter** to the First Bank of the United States. A charter is an agreement that grants a person or organization special rights and privileges. Even though the bank did a good job of supplying currency and acting as the government's banker, when the time came to renew the charter, Congress refused to do so. Without a central bank for the entire country, banking became the responsibility of the individual states.

The first national money system was set up in 1792. The Coinage Act made the dollar the basic unit of money, and gold and silver were declared legal money.

State-Chartered Banks

As the United States continued to expand, American businesses began to grow. Settlers built new towns, roads, schools, and railroads. Farmers produced more crops

The First Bank of the United States was established in Philadelphia, Pennsylvania, in 1791.

and livestock and sold them in markets. The number of banks grew as well. State-approved financial institutions took deposits in the form of gold and silver and made loans using their own bank notes. Banks were required by state law to keep a certain amount of precious metal on reserve to give to customers who wanted to exchange, or redeem, the bank notes for gold and silver. The banks would then lend or **invest** any money they had left over. They invested money by buying parts of new businesses, which helped them grow.

This system worked well as long as depositors were confident that the bank could make good on its promise to redeem bank notes for gold or silver. Bankers prominently displayed their gold and silver reserves in vaults with glass doors so that customers could see the money.

Customers depended on state governments to make sure that financial institutions kept the required amount of reserves and were run honestly. That didn't always happen. When people lost confidence in a financial institution, they would panic and quickly run to get their gold or silver out of the bank before it closed. That's how the phrases "bank run" and "bank panic" originated.

In this newspaper drawing from the mid-1800s, gold miners in Colorado brought gold dust into the "banking-house" to be weighed.

A Second Central Bank

By the early 1800s, bank failures were common. There was no common currency in the country. Hundreds of financial institutions issued their own currency. The money that people received from one bank looked completely different from money issued by another bank! Merchants had to use a directory to check whether or not the money their customers wanted to use was worth anything. If the bank that issued the note didn't have a good reputation, merchants either did not accept the note or accepted it for only part of its value.

Some dishonest bankers took people's money in exchange for bank notes and then promptly closed. Others misrepresented the amount of gold or silver they kept on reserve by covering the top of a barrel of nails with gold or silver coins.

Once again, Congress decided to establish a central bank. In 1816 the Second Bank of the United States was chartered. Critics felt that the Second Bank did not issue enough currency. They worried that lack of abundant currency would limit trade. When the charter for the Second Bank came up for renewal in 1836, Congress voted against it.

The National Banking Act

The United States continued to expand and grow rapidly. Improved transportation methods, such as railroads and steamboats, and better transportation routes increased the need for a common currency among a growing number of merchants, farmers, and craftspeople.

In the meantime, state banks continued to issue their

In the 1800s, several kinds of bank notes were in circulation, creating confusion for merchants.

own currencies. By the start of the Civil War, in 1861, there were 10,000 different types of bank notes in circulation. Merchants and store owners would only accept the currency they were familiar with. Not only were individuals having problems paying for goods and services, but the government was as well.

The government had to find a way to pay for the expenses of the Civil War. The country needed a currency that everyone would accept. In response, the government issued new, fiat money. People called these bills "greenbacks," because the backs were printed in green ink.

People crowded outside a bank during an 1893 bank run.

Then, in 1864, President Abraham Lincoln signed the National Banking Act. This act established the position of comptroller of the currency—the person who was responsible for issuing the country's first national bank notes. These notes were given to banks with national bank charters—those authorized by the federal government.

The U.S. Treasury designated this national currency legal tender, which meant it was good for paying all taxes and debts. As national notes became widely accepted, greenbacks and notes issued by individual state banks disappeared.

While the National Banking Act resolved some of the country's banking troubles, problems remained. Financial institutions in small towns and cities often sent their reserve deposits to larger banks in New York, Chicago, or St. Louis. When the small banks experienced high demand for cash, they couldn't always get their money back quickly enough to meet customer demand. The news would quickly spread, and the banks experienced runs on deposits.

The Panic of 1907

In 1907 the U.S. banking system reached a breaking point. Between 1897 and 1907, the number of state-chartered financial institutions had grown very rapidly. These financial institutions did not have to meet the same reserve requirements established for nationally chartered banks under the National Banking Act. Without any government control, the state institutions were only as stable and safe as the people who were running them.

In addition, many banks invested heavily in **stocks**—

shares of ownership in corporations. When the price of stocks took an unexpected sharp decline in October 1907, the banks suffered large losses. As a result, financial institutions could not give all of their customers the money they had deposited.

Some of these customers included smaller banks that had deposited reserves in the larger banks. The crisis spread throughout the country. Small banks could not get funds from the large banks to meet their customer demands. Many banks had to close their doors. Thousands of depositors lost money.

The bank failures prompted Congress to establish the National Monetary Commission in 1907. This group was told to study the problems and suggest possible ways to steady the country's banking system. It recommended that another central bank be formed.

The central bank would be responsible for assuring a stable currency that could be adjusted to meet the nation's needs. The central bank would also supervise nationally chartered banks. Six years later, the Federal Reserve Bank was established.

The Great Depression

Another crisis hit the U.S. banking system in 1929. That year the stock market crashed, and many people who had invested in stocks lost their investments. Businesses found that people were not buying products and services. Without sales, many businesses had to close their doors and lay off their employees. Thousands of workers were without jobs.

People panicked. They ran to banks to withdraw their

savings. But when so many people went to withdraw the money they had deposited in financial institutions all at once, the financial institutions could not meet their demands.

The banks had not kept all of the money in vaults, but had lent it to other customers. Just as in 1907, some financial institutions had also invested some of their deposits in the stock market. When the crash of 1929 came, that money was lost as well.

To help restore people's confidence in banks and other financial institutions, Congress made sweeping changes in the banking system. In 1933 it created the Federal Deposit Insurance Corporation (FDIC) to insure customers' deposits. The FDIC insures depositors' money up to $100,000. If your financial institution fails, you will get back all of the money you deposited, up to $100,000 per account.

Alternatives to Banks

During the early 1800s, new kinds of financial institutions began operating. Banks mainly dealt with business customers and wealthy individuals.

Mutual Savings Banks

In 1816 mutual savings societies in Philadelphia and Boston began offering financial services to working-class individuals. The term *mutual* means that the savings society was owned (mutually) by the depositors. The mutuals, which acted like banks, made it possible for people with small amounts of money to keep it in a safe place and earn interest on their savings.

Savings and Loans

The Oxford Provident Building Association in Philadelphia opened its doors as the country's first savings and loan association in 1831. Savings and loans (often referred to as S & Ls) were originally established to lend money to customers who wanted to buy a home. Like mutual savings banks, these institutions were intended to help working-class savers.

Credit Unions

Credit unions have been around since 1909. They are usually formed by a group of people with a common bond, such as the same place of employment. Credit unions are somewhat like clubs where members can go to get the same services offered by other financial institutions.

Because the purpose of a credit union is to serve its members, it will often give a loan to a member when another financial institution would not. For instance, a credit union may be more willing than a bank to give a loan to someone who has never borrowed money before.

Modern Banking

In 1980 Congress revised many of the banking rules that had been put in place after the Great Depression. Congress passed the Depository Institutions Deregulation and Monetary Control Act of 1980. The act removed some of the restrictions that had been placed on financial institutions regarding the kinds of services and interest rates they could offer.

This legislation was meant to allow financial institutions to compete more easily for customer deposits and

After the Monetary Control Act of 1980, stockbrokers could compete with traditional banks to provide financial services.

loans. Since then financial institutions have had more freedom to set interest rates and offer a wide variety of services. The new regulations covered banks, savings and loan associations, and credit unions.

As a result of these changes, financial institutions aggressively compete for customer deposits and loans. While some consumers have benefited by receiving higher interest rates on savings accounts, lower interest rates on loans, and improved services, this competition also led to the failure of many financial institutions during the 1980s, particularly in the savings and loan industry.

Many financial institutions loaned money to people who couldn't repay their loans, or paid savers interest rates that were too high. In some cases the S & Ls were poorly managed or run by dishonest people.

Fortunately, people who deposited money in savings and loans did not lose their money. Similar to the FDIC, the Federal Savings and Loan Insurance Corporation (FSLIC) insures the money of savings and loan depositors. Because of widespread mismanagement and illegal financial activities in the savings and loan industry, however, the FSLIC could not cover all the funds that were lost. During 1989 and 1990, Congress had to take steps to bail out the failed S & Ls to keep people confident in the banking system. U.S. taxpayers will have to make up the difference between what the FSLIC can pay and what is owed to depositors.

The FSLIC has been merged with the FDIC in order to better monitor savings and loans. New, tougher requirements have been set for savings and loans to ensure financial stability.

Different Kinds of Financial Institutions

As consumers of financial services, we have more choices than ever before. We have a wide variety of options when it comes to saving, investing, and borrowing money.

Depository Institutions

Banks, savings and loan associations, and credit unions are all considered **depository institutions**. They take consumer deposits in two basic forms. Checking

This bank in Owatonna, Minnesota, was designed by architect Louis Sullivan and built in 1907. Many depository institutions are noted for their interesting architecture.

accounts are known as demand-deposit accounts. Money can be withdrawn at any time—on demand. Most consumers use checking accounts for day-to-day payments. Savings or time-deposit accounts are offered to consumers who want to deposit money for longer periods of time. Depository institutions use customer deposits to make loans to consumers and businesses.

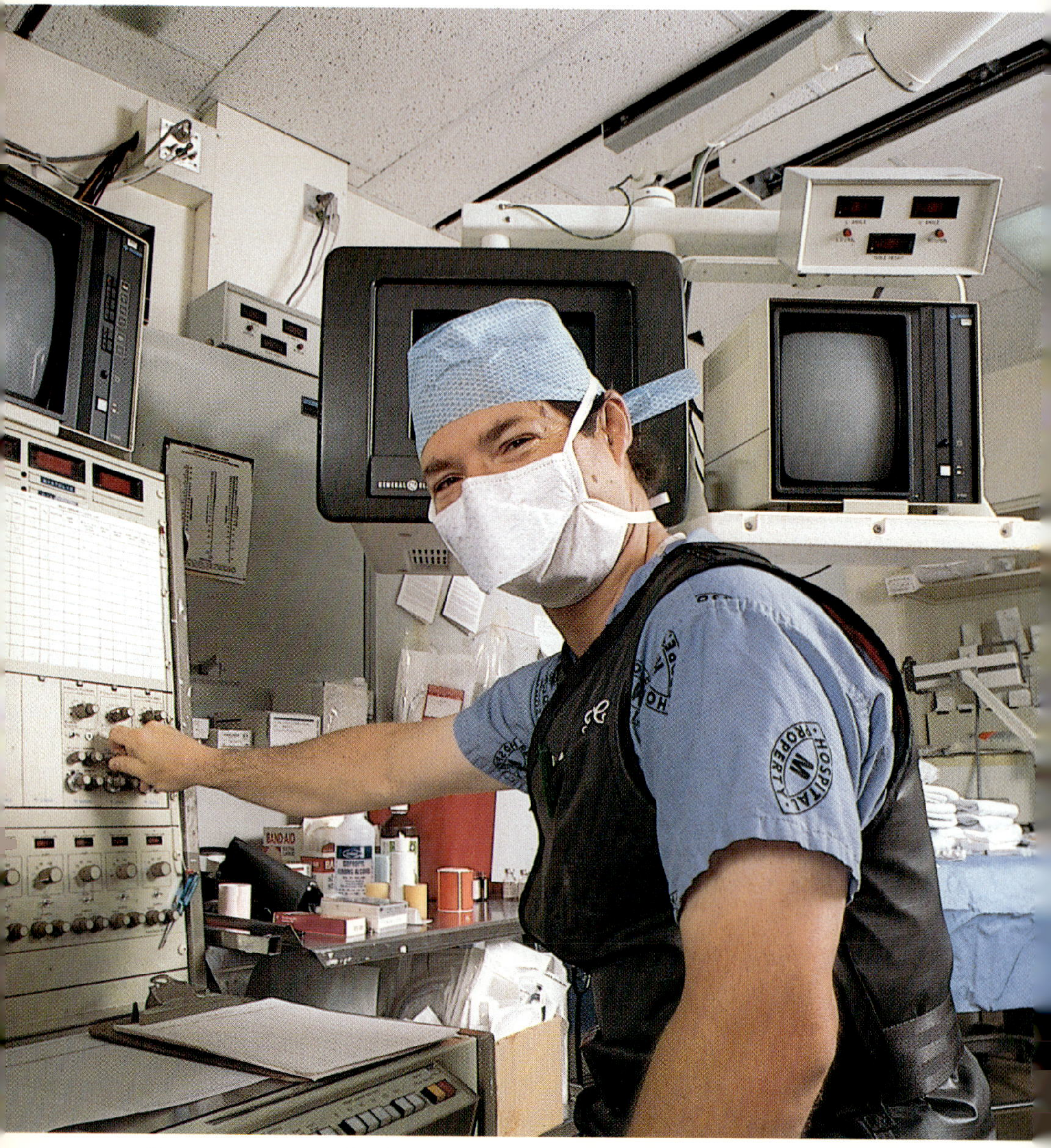

Insurance companies help people in case of hardship, like a hospital stay. Insurance companies are a kind of contractual institution.

Just like goldsmiths in earlier times, financial institutions still offer safekeeping services for customers' valuables, such as stock certificates, jewelry, and rare objects, which are kept in safe-deposit boxes for a fee.

Contractual Institutions

Contractual institutions such as insurance companies offer financial services for specific needs or events. People buy insurance to protect against future hardship. For example, when you buy health insurance, you pay the insurance company a certain amount of money each year. Then if you get sick and have to go into a hospital, the insurance company pays most or part of the bill. Common kinds of insurance include health insurance, life insurance, fire insurance, car insurance, and home insurance. Insurance companies invest the money customers pay them.

Investment Companies

Investments, as opposed to savings, are for customers who are willing to take more risks in exchange for the possibility of getting more money back than they could from the interest payments offered by banks and other depository institutions. Through investment companies, people buy stocks and **bonds**. In return for investing in corporations, customers hope to receive money at some point in the future.

Investment companies make investments that they believe will earn high rates of return. If the companies that they have invested in grow and make a profit, customers receive a portion of the profits. But if the companies don't do well, customers can lose the money they invested.

If you buy a new car, one way you could get a loan is through a finance company.

If a company goes broke, the investors' stock will be worthless.

Finance Companies

Finance companies offer an alternative to borrowing money from more traditional financial institutions, such as banks, savings and loan associations, or credit unions. Finance companies typically make people meet fewer requirements to get a loan. However, interest rates charged by finance companies are sometimes higher than those of other financial institutions. It's always a good idea to compare rates before getting a loan.

Some finance companies give loans for specific types of purchases, such as furniture or cars. For instance, many large car makers, such as General Motors, also own a finance company. When you want to buy a new car, the car dealership can offer you a loan for the car as well. If you buy a GM car, for example, you could get a loan through the General Motors Assurance Corporation (GMAC).

THE FEDERAL RESERVE: THE BANKERS' BANK

In 1913 the Federal Reserve Bank—often called just the Fed—was established. Its purpose was to help provide a flexible, adequate supply of currency, to assure citizens that the country's banking system was sound, and to promote a healthy economy. These things sound good—after all, no one wants an unhealthy economy! But what is a healthy economy anyway?

A Healthy Economy

When people talk about a "healthy economy," they usually

5

mean growth, stable prices, high employment, and a secure financial system.

Economic growth happens when businesses become more productive. Being more productive means finding a better or less expensive way of doing something. Here's an example of how this works.

As a member of the Jones family, Jerrold is responsible for providing snow-shoveling services to the household. He's not thrilled about this responsibility, but it's part of being in a family. Every time it snows, Jerrold is expected to shovel the sidewalk and driveway before he leaves for school.

One day, Jerrold makes a discovery. By adding strips of metal to each side of his shovel, he can finish shoveling the sidewalk and driveway more quickly. In fact, he has enough time left to shovel his neighbor's sidewalk and driveway, too. His neighbor is willing to pay Jerrold $5 for performing the service.

Jerrold's invention has made him more productive. He has extra time to shovel the neighbor's sidewalk and driveway and he can earn money doing it. This same concept can happen on a larger scale.

When a business finds ways to be more productive, it can do more things or make more goods and earn more money. As a result, the business can hire more people. These people spend their earnings on food, clothing, housing, cars, haircuts, movies, and so on. Part of people's earnings can also be saved for future purchases.

To be more productive, Jerrold had to improve his shoveling system. First he had to think of the idea and then he had to invest in metal strips to improve his shovel. That cost Jerrold brainpower—and money. Jerrold didn't have any money of his own, so he went to the only place he knew would lend him money, the Bank of Jones—also known as Jerrold's mom. After Jerrold discussed his idea with his "banker," Ms. Jones felt confident that the money she lent her son would be put to productive use and Jerrold would be able to repay his loan. So she lent him the money.

Ms. Jones was able to lend her son money because the Jones family had *saved* money. Businesses get money to improve or develop new products and services by going to banks and borrowing money—money deposited in banks by people who save.

What would have happened if the Bank of Jones didn't give Jerrold a loan? Jerrold wouldn't have had the money to add the metal strips to his shovel. He wouldn't have been able to improve his productivity. He wouldn't have been able to earn any more money, so he wouldn't have been able to spend or save the $5 per snowfall he earned from the neighbor. In short, there wouldn't have been any economic growth.

This example shows how money is involved in helping an economy grow—money makes goods move. The story also points out the importance of both spending and saving. You can't have one without the other. Finally, Jerrold's example shows what happens if money isn't available. With no money to get his project off the ground, he can't act on his good idea and has to continue shoveling the old way. The neighbor must hire someone else to shovel his sidewalk. And the stores or financial institutions where Jerrold would have spent or saved his extra money suffer because they don't get new business.

Another sign of a healthy economy is stable prices.

High employment and business growth are two signs of a healthy economy.

This means that your money will buy the same amount of goods and services a year from now as it can today. Stable prices are especially important for people who have to live on the same income, or earnings, from year to year, such as retired people. If inflation occurs and prices increase—a bag of groceries that costs $15 this year costs $25 next year, for example—then retired people may have a hard time affording basic necessities.

Employment is also crucial to the economy. High employment means that all people who want a job have one. If people can't find work, they can't afford to pay for their basic needs like food, clothing, and housing. When large numbers of people are without jobs, businesses also suffer, because people can't afford to spend money on new cars, eating out, going to a movie, and other things. Everyone suffers when unemployment is high.

Trying to maintain a healthy economy is a balancing act. Too much money in the economy can be just as bad for consumers as too little money in the economy. With too much money in the economy, people want to buy more and more goods and services. Demand goes up, and businesses can charge higher prices, because consumers have more money to pay for items. When inflation causes prices to go up, though, the purchasing power of money goes down. That means that a dollar will buy less than it did before.

Economists—people who study the economy for a living—try to predict what consumers and businesses want and need to maintain a healthy, growing economy. One of the organizations that plays a key role in helping to keep the supply of money at just the right level is the "keeper of the money"—the Federal Reserve Bank.

The Central Bank

The Federal Reserve Bank is made up of representatives from all areas of the United States, so that each region can have input into the country's economic policy. The Federal Reserve is run by a chairperson and a board of governors in Washington, D.C. The chair of the Federal Reserve is appointed by the president and serves a four-year term. Federal Reserve board members are appointed by the president and confirmed by the Senate. Each board member serves a 14-year term.

Twelve regional reserve banks offer advice to the board of governors and provide banking services to the financial institutions in their Federal Reserve district. Federal Reserve banks are located in Boston, New York, Philadelphia, Cleveland, Richmond, Atlanta, Chicago, St. Louis, Minneapolis, Kansas City, Dallas, and San Francisco.

The Federal Reserve Bank of New York; pictured on page 59 is the Federal Reserve Bank of Minneapolis.

Each regional reserve bank holds member banks' reserves—the amount of money that each bank is required to keep on hand to meet customers' withdrawal needs. If a financial institution experiences a great demand for money, it can borrow additional funds from the Federal Reserve.

The Functions of the Federal Reserve

The Federal Reserve Bank has three major responsibilities: monetary policy, supervision and regulation, and financial services.

Monetary Policy

One reason the Federal Reserve was formed was to help create and maintain a steady, growing economy, stable prices, and high employment. It tries to achieve this goal through its monetary policy activities. Monetary policy refers to the Fed's approach to keeping the economy healthy by controlling the supply of money.

Every month, the presidents of the regional banks and the Federal Reserve board of governors meet to discuss monetary policy. By influencing the ability of financial institutions to lend money, the Fed can expand or reduce the **money supply**—the amount of money in the economy. The Fed uses three tools to do this: open market operations, reserve requirements, and the discount rate.

Open Market Operations

The Federal Reserve's most powerful tool to influence

U.S. Treasury bonds help pay for public goods such as new highways.

the economy is its open market operations. Eight times each year, a committee called the Federal Open Market Committee (FOMC) meets to review the condition of the economy and decide if the Federal Reserve should act to speed up or slow down the economy.

The FOMC is made up of 5 of the 12 Federal Reserve Bank regional presidents and the 7 members of the board of governors. The main activity of the FOMC is to buy or sell U.S. **Treasury bonds**.

U.S. Treasury bonds (also called T bills) represent government debt. The U.S. Treasury sells bonds as one way to get the money it needs to pay for public goods (taxes are another way that the government earns money). Public goods include services such as defense, medical programs for old or poor people, food, clothing, and shelter for poor people, new highways, clean air, and police protection.

When people buy U.S. Treasury bonds—bonds can be purchased through investment companies or directly from the Treasury—they are lending money to the government. In return, the government will repay investors the amount of the loan, plus interest. This is similar to how banks lend money to consumers and businesses.

Taking into account several factors, the FOMC decides whether it needs to add money to or take money out of the economy. If the committee decides to *increase* the supply of money, it buys U.S. Treasury bonds in the open market—that is, from investment companies. If the FOMC decides that it needs to *tighten* the supply of money in the economy, it sells bonds.

When the Fed sells bonds, consumers and businesses pay for the bonds by taking money out of their financial institution accounts. In turn, financial institutions have less money available to lend. When the Fed buys bonds, it pays for them by depositing money into financial institution accounts. Then the financial institutions have more money to lend.

Reserve Requirements

Financial institutions must keep a certain amount of money on reserve—or on account—with the Federal Reserve. The amount depends on the institution's size and the types of deposits it has. Demand—or checking—deposits require one level of reserves, while time—or savings—deposits have different reserve requirements.

Up until 1980, only member banks were required to maintain reserves at the Fed. The Monetary Control Act requires that all depository institutions (banks, savings and loan associations, and credit unions) follow the Fed's reserve requirements. This change in the law has increased the Fed's control over the money supply.

The Fed monitors each financial institution's reserve position daily. Money over and above an institution's reserve requirement can be lent to consumers and businesses.

For example, if a bank is required to keep 10 percent of its deposits on reserve, it can lend the remaining 90 percent to borrowers. For every $100 the bank has in deposits, it would be required to keep $10 in reserve at the Fed. The bank would have $90 available to lend to qualified borrowers.

If the Fed decided that financial institutions had to keep 20 percent of deposits on reserve, then they would have only $80 of every $100 in deposits to lend to customers. The remaining $20 would have to be held in a reserve account at the Fed. Less money would be available for consumers and businesses that wanted to borrow money.

The Fed might increase reserve requirements when it decides that prices are rising too quickly and it must tighten, or reduce, the money supply. When reserve requirements go up, the cost of borrowing money increases. Financial institutions have less money available to lend, and fewer consumers and businesses can afford to borrow money. When a product (in this case money) becomes scarce, its price increases.

Suppose you collect baseball cards. When there are thousands of a certain baseball card, the price that you have to pay for it is relatively low. Since they are easy to

10% Reserve Requirement

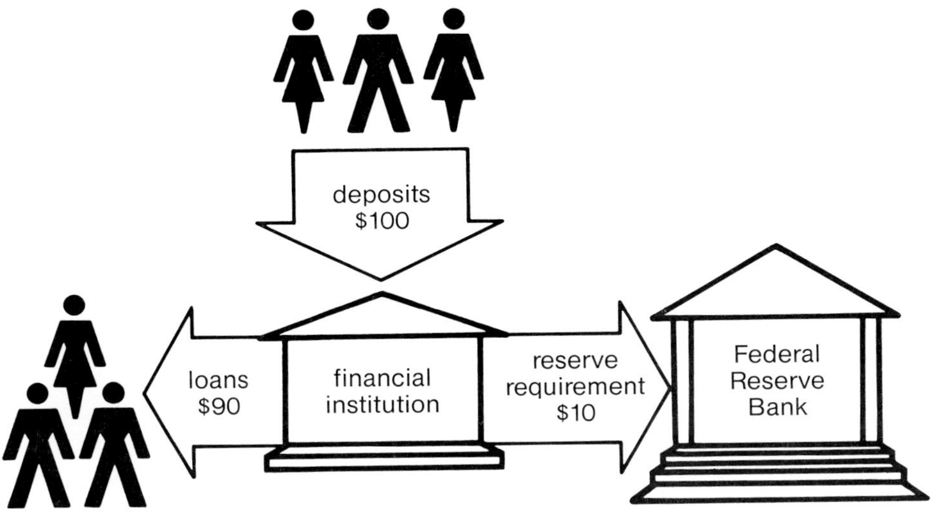

Reserve requirements affect the amount of money financial institutions have available to lend to customers.

get, people will not pay a lot for them. But when you want to acquire a Ty Cobb baseball card, which is extremely rare, you'll have to pay a high price. The fewer items there are available, the higher the price will be.

The same concept holds true when money is scarce—or tight. The price you have to pay—the interest rate—will be high. The higher the price of an item, the fewer people there are willing to pay for it.

On the other hand, if the Fed wants to stimulate—or increase—growth, it can lower the reserve requirement. The Fed may decide to do this because it feels that business growth is slow or employment rates are too low. When the Fed lowers reserve requirements, the price of money—the interest rate—goes down. Financial institutions then have more money available to lend to consumers and businesses, at prices they can afford.

With more money available to lend, financial institutions would be able to offer loans to consumers and businesses at lower interest rates. More consumers and businesses would be willing and able to borrow money to buy new cars, build new homes, or improve manufacturing plants.

The Fed carefully considers when to raise or lower reserve requirements. The raising or lowering of reserve requirements can make front-page news, since the change sends a message to consumers and businesses about what the "experts" at the Fed think is happening in the economy.

The Discount Rate

A final tool that the Fed carries in its "monetary policy tool bag" is the **discount rate**. The discount rate is the price—or interest rate—that financial institutions must pay to borrow money from the Federal Reserve.

Borrowing from the Fed is often referred to as "going to the discount window." The phrase stems from the days when bankers went into a Federal Reserve bank and borrowed money from a person who stood behind some sort of protective window. Now going to the discount window can be done using electronic funds transfer and the telephone.

The Fed acts as a lender of last resort to financial institutions in need of funds. This service helps citizens feel confident in the country's financial system, because we know that if a financial institution finds itself in trouble, it can turn to the Fed for help.

The discount rate helps financial institutions handle the ups and downs of their deposit and loan demands. For instance, a financial institution may find that a

Banks and other financial institutions rely on the Fed to handle their customers' currency and coin demands.

larger than expected number of customers are taking money out of their accounts on a given day. The financial institution could borrow money from the Fed to meet its reserve requirements.

If the discount rate is high, financial institutions think twice about making loans. If a financial institution has to borrow money from the Fed to meet reserve requirements, the cost is high. However, if the Fed lowers the discount rate, financial institutions would be more likely to make more loans to customers, because the cost of borrowing from the Fed would be less.

Like reserve requirements, many economists view the discount rate as a sign of how the Fed feels about the economy. The Federal Reserve is very careful about changing the discount rate because it wants to send the right message to consumers and businesses about the health of the economy.

Supervision and Regulation

A second function of the Federal Reserve is to supervise and regulate banks and other financial institutions. Federal Reserve employees regularly review financial institution records, operations, and procedures to make sure that they are maintaining the proper reserve requirements and following all banking rules.

You can think of the Fed's supervision and regulation activities like regular dental checkups—except that financial institutions are required by law to have regular exams! Federal Reserve Bank examiners check up on financial institutions to make certain that money is handled properly.

Financial Services

One of the original reasons that the Federal Reserve Bank was formed was to provide financial services to banks, and later to all financial institutions. As the bankers' bank, the Fed provides the same types of services consumers get from their financial institutions. But you could not deposit money at a Federal Reserve Bank. That privilege is reserved for banks, savings and loan associations, and credit unions.

The Federal Reserve is also in charge of distributing new coin and currency. Reserve banks order currency and coin from the U.S. Treasury. In turn, financial institutions order currency and coin from their local reserve bank.

Institutions also deposit currency and coin at the Fed. When cash is deposited, it is counted, examined to make certain that it is not counterfeit, and checked for fitness. If the currency is torn or soiled, it is destroyed and replaced with new, fit currency.

The Federal Reserve also acts as a central check-clearing facility. In 1988 the Federal Reserve system handled 15.3 billion checks valued at $10.3 trillion.

The Fed earns money by charging service fees to financial institutions, collecting interest on loans made to financial institutions, and earning interest on government bonds. If the Fed earns more money than it needs to cover its costs, it turns the money over to the U.S. Treasury.

When the Federal Reserve was established, its main priority was to provide the U.S. with a flexible supply of money. Over the years, the Fed's responsibilities have changed as the country's needs have changed.

When it arrives at the Fed, currency is checked to make sure it's in good condition.

MONEY SUPPLY: MAKING MONEY

When we talk about "making money," most of us understand it to mean that we will get paid a certain sum of money for a job or service we perform. When people ask you, "How much money do you make?" they are inquiring about how much money you earn.

The U.S. Treasury literally "makes money," while counterfeiters "make money" illegally. Economists use the phrase "making money" in yet another way. They mean increasing the supply of money in the economy, or creating new money. Adding to the

6

money supply is an important—and somewhat perplexing—job. And each of us helps in this process of "making money." Let's look at an example of how this works.

Katie Gets New Wheels

On the first day that First National Bank opened for business, consumers and businesses deposited a total of $10,000 in the bank. The customers expect that in exchange for the money they deposited, they will earn interest. To meet that expectation, First National has to use the deposits to make more money.

According to Federal Reserve requirements, First National must hold 20 percent, or $2,000, of its deposits in reserve. With $2,000 in its Fed account, the bank has $8,000 left over that it can lend to customers. This portion of the depositors' money will be used to make more money in order to pay interest to depositors and to cover the costs of running a bank.

At the same time that people were depositing money at First National, Katie Smith was meeting with a banker to discuss her need for a new car. After deciding that Katie would be able to repay the loan, First National put $8,000 into Katie's checking account. They also agreed on a payment schedule that included monthly payments for the principal (the $8,000) and the interest Katie would pay as a fee for borrowing money.

Delighted, Katie left the bank and went directly to the car dealership. After some wheeling and dealing, Katie and the salesperson agreed on a price for the car. Katie wrote out a check payable to the car dealership for

$8,000. Everyone was happy. Katie drove away with her new car, the salesperson made a sale, and the bank was glad to have made a loan to Katie. The interest she will pay for borrowing money will help the bank pay depositors their interest fee for keeping money at First National.

But the story doesn't end with Katie getting a new car. At the end of the day, the car dealership deposited Ms. Smith's check in the dealership's checking account at Super Saver Savings and Loan. Super Saver now has an additional $8,000 in deposits. After putting 20 percent of the money in Super Saver's reserve account at the Fed, Super Saver now has $6,400 to lend or invest.

Rudy Buys a French Fryer

It's lucky that Super Saver has money to lend, since Rudy's Really Great Burgers' french fry machine just fried its last french fry. Rudy explains to the loan officer at Super Saver S & L that his restaurant needs a new french fryer.

After making sure that Rudy can repay the S & L, Super Saver lends Rudy $6,400 to purchase a new high-tech french fry machine. Super Saver enters $6,400 into Rudy's checking account. Rudy then writes a check to the New-Fangled Fryer Company for $6,400. No currency exchanges hands. Amounts of money are simply added or subtracted from one account to another.

The New-Fangled Fryer Company takes the check that Rudy wrote for the new fryer and deposits it in the checking account it maintains at Fry-Makers National Credit Union. The reserve and lending process continues. Fry-Makers National Credit Union deposits

Making Money

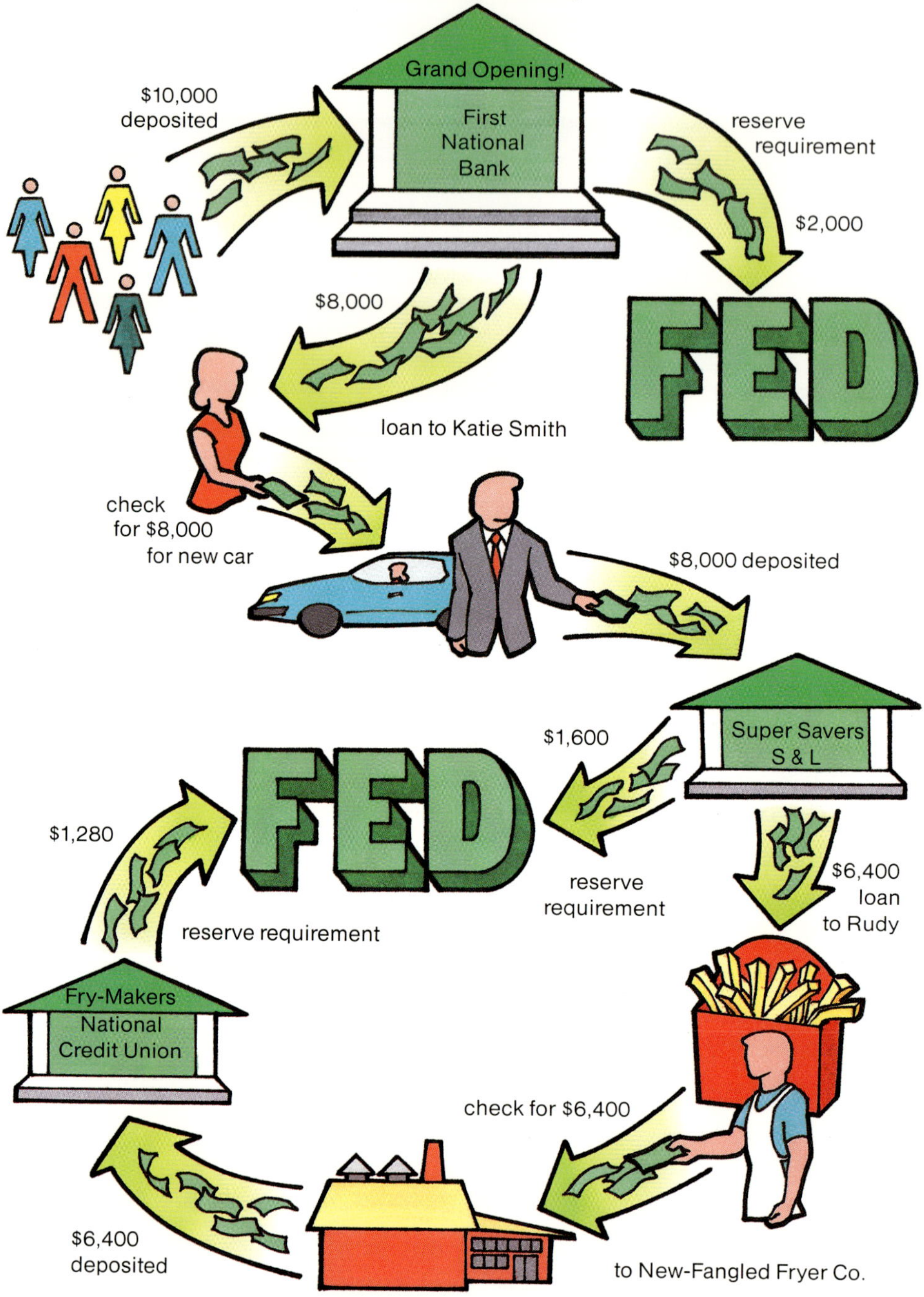

$1,280 (20 percent of $6,400) to its Fed account and now has $5,120 available to lend.

$10,000 Makes $19,520

Do you see what's happening? The original $10,000 that consumers deposited in First National has increased the general money supply by $19,520: $8,000 + $6,400 + $5,120. The money has grown because checks are deposited in banks, rather than cashed. With more deposits, financial institutions have more money to lend or invest. It's the same concept that the goldsmiths used in the Middle Ages. Financial institutions trust that not all depositors are going to withdraw their money at the same time. So they keep a small reserve on hand and use the rest of the money to lend or invest.

If the Federal Reserve wasn't satisfied with the condition of the economy, it might decide to tighten, or slow, the growth of the money supply. One way that it could do this would be to increase reserve requirements. Let's go back to the example above and see what would happen if reserve requirements were increased to 25 percent.

Tight Money

With a 25 percent reserve requirement, First National Bank would have $7,500 available to lend to consumers or businesses. Katie Smith would only be able to borrow $7,500 from First National for her car. If she wanted to purchase an $8,000 car, she would either have to find another source for additional funds or buy a less expensive car. Say that Katie decides to buy a less expensive car.

Katie pays $7,500 to the dealership. In turn, the dealership deposits $7,500 into Super Saver Savings and Loan. After adding $1,875 to its Fed reserve account, the financial institution has $5,625 available to lend to Rudy's Really Great Burgers. Since Super Saver only has $5,625 to lend, Rudy decides to buy a cheaper french fry machine. A better machine would cost $6,400 and money is "too tight" to get a loan for that amount.

The $5,625 that Rudy paid for the french fry machine is deposited into Fry-Makers National Credit Union, which then begins to find borrowers for $4,218.75, the amount available after the 25 percent reserve requirement is deducted.

The amount of money created with an increased reserve requirement is less: $17,343.75 ($7,500 + $5,625 + $4,218.75). The money supply slows when reserve requirements go up and grows when reserve requirements go down.

Making Adjustments

The Federal Reserve continually monitors the health of the economy. It then uses its three basic monetary tools to make adjustments. The three tools, discussed in chapter 5, include buying and selling bonds through the Federal Open Market Committee, raising or lowering the discount rate, and raising or lowering reserve requirements.

Because our economy is complex and can be affected by many factors, the Fed's tools are sometimes not very precise. Economists and monetary policymakers—those who help make decisions about how the Fed should respond to economic changes—spend a great deal of time analyzing how best to maintain a healthy, growing, stable economy. Economists try to develop theories that will help predict the turns and changes in the economy.

It is this continual change that keeps economists as well as consumers interested in the economy. The economy affects how each of us spends and invests our hard-earned money.

7

THE FUTURE OF FINANCIAL INSTITUTIONS

One of the driving forces behind the forms that money takes and how money is used has been technology. New technology—which includes new inventions, discoveries, tools, and techniques—changes the way people do business, including banking. As transportation improved, the ability to trade expanded. People needed a "transportable" form of money. As economies developed, the use of commodity money and currency and coin decreased and the use of checks and electronic funds transfer increased.

Computing Cash

Now telecommunications and advanced computer systems are changing financial institutions into information processors and money into electronic blips. Instead of people physically exchanging money, entries are made in a computer system. On a computer, money is given to—credited—or taken from—debited—a checking or savings account. The trend of electronic payments will continue.

For example, Mark belongs to a health club that charges him $30 a month for membership. Mark has an agreement with his bank that the bank will automatically deduct—debit--the $30 from his checking account each month to pay the club. Mark does not have to go to the club and pay his dues. He doesn't have anything to do with the transaction, except to make certain he has enough money in his account to make the payment and to note that the money was taken out of his checking account when he gets a statement of his account.

Businesses have been making payments by crediting and debiting bank accounts for some time. Governmental organizations are beginning to do the same thing. Several states require that business tax payments be made using electronic payment methods. The Internal Revenue Service is testing the use of electronic payment methods as a way to make tax refunds. Traditionally, refund checks have been sent in the mail.

Financial institutions rely on elaborate check-clearing and transportation systems to handle the millions of checks they receive each day. This expensive and time-consuming process could change with new technology that is being tested by the Federal Reserve. Electronically

Checks are sorted by a machine (above)*, then organized by workers. Processing checks is time-consuming and expensive. Electronic check-clearing could make the job easier in the future.*

Unlike U.S. currency, British and German currency is printed in different colors.

clearing checks would allow financial institutions to transmit images, or pictures, of checks for payment, rather than having to present the actual paper check.

Plastic Money

When most people talk about "plastic money," they are referring to credit cards. But in the Cocos Islands, the islanders actually use money made of plastic. In the past, their coins were made of ivory. Then they began using plastic made to look like ivory. The U.S. government has thought about using plastic coins.

Foiling Fakers

The U.S. government tries to find ways to make counterfeiting money more difficult. American money is the only money in the world that is printed in just one color, no matter what the dollar amount of the bill. This makes U.S. money an easy target for counterfeiters, since they only have to reproduce one color of ink.

The Bureau of Engraving and Printing is experimenting with a variety of ways to outsmart counterfeiters. The bureau is considering weaving a polyester thread inside the paper that would spell out the dollar amount as part of the bill. Another idea is to incorporate a metal thread into the currency. British currency uses such a thread. The U.S. Treasury is also considering putting holograms—three-dimensional pictures—on bills.

It's in the Cards

When you pay for things with a credit card, you receive a monthly bill that lists all the charges you made. A debit card looks and acts like a credit card. You are not billed monthly, however. Your purchases are automatically deducted, or debited, from your checking account. Each month debit card users receive a statement listing both the checks they wrote and the times they used their debit card.

Financial institutions also provide consumers with an easy way to get cash or make deposits 24 hours a day with automated teller machines, or ATMs. Using an ATM card with a personal identification number (PIN), consumers can gain access to their checking or savings account.

It's a Super Card!

In France, consumers are using a special debit card to make purchases. The card, called Supercard, looks like a credit card, but it has a computer microchip in it. Stored on the chip is all sorts of information about the cardholder, such as name, address, date of birth, medical information, the amount of money in the person's bank account, driver's license number, and more. The Supercard can be used just like a debit card. The card can even be used at pay telephones and in buses or subways.

Account Information at Your Fingertips

Many financial institutions also allow customers to find out account information through a new technique called automated response units. Using a touch-tone telephone, consumers can get information about their savings and checking accounts. Customers can also transfer money between their checking and savings accounts over the telephone.

It's a Small, Smaller World

In a very real way, the world is becoming a smaller place. The United States is dependent on trade with countries throughout the world. Technology has helped streamline the way that businesses pay their foreign trading partners. Computer software systems help translate U.S. currency into the foreign currency equivalents and then electronically send payments through international wire transfer systems.

Foreign trade has also meant more competition among

In the future, people will do more of their banking over the phone.

financial institutions. U.S. financial institutions must compete with foreign banks. Some financial institutions will go out of business if they can't compete.

It's easy to look at the history of money and the role that it's played and think that there isn't any more room for change. But money has always changed to meet the needs of the people who use it. Since people will never stop changing, neither will money!

GLOSSARY

barter—the direct exchange of goods without the use of money

bills of exchange—written agreements outlining what two trading partners would accept as payment

bond—a loan of money to a company, organization, or government

central bank—a bank that regulates a country's financial institutions and controls its money supply

charter—a written agreement or contract that gives a person or organization special rights and privileges

check—written instructions from an account holder at a financial institution to pay a sum of money to the person or organization designated

collateral—goods or property owned by a borrower that a financial institution could sell if the borrower fails to repay a loan

commodity money—agricultural or natural resources used as a medium of exchange

counterfeit—fake or imitation money

credit—a way of delaying payment for goods and services until a later time

credit card—a plastic card used as money to "charge" goods and services; interest is charged for the use of the card if the charges are not repaid in full each month.

currency—the money that circulates within a country; currency usually refers to paper money.

debit card—a plastic card used as money; funds are drawn from a person's checking account.

denomination—the value, or dollar amount, of a bill or coin

depository institutions—financial institutions that offer checking and savings accounts; includes banks, credit unions, and savings and loan associations.

discount rate—the price, or interest rate, that financial institutions must pay to borrow money from the Federal Reserve Bank

durable goods—goods that last a long time, such as automobiles and houses

Federal Reserve—the central bank of the United States

Federal Reserve note—United States currency

fiat money—money that does not have value in and of itself or is not backed by something of value

fractional reserve system—the technique used by financial institutions of keeping a fraction of money on reserve for customers' cash needs and lending the remaining money to borrowers

gold-backed—money that can be exchanged for an equal amount of gold upon request

inflation—a continual rise in the average price of goods and services

installment—a portion of a loan that is repaid periodically, usually once a month

interest—a fee charged for borrowing money or earned for saving money

interest rate—the amount of money it costs to borrow money expressed as a percentage, or the amount of money paid for saving, expressed as a percentage.

invest—to buy a part of a business in the hope of earning more money in return

legal tender—money that has been declared acceptable by a government for payment of debts

letter of credit—a document that states the amount of money a person has in storage and verifies the person's ability to pay for goods and services

liquid—items that can quickly and easily be converted into legal tender or cash

loan—money that is borrowed with a promise to repay the money at an agreed-upon time and interest rate

medium of exchange—something that is used to pay for goods and services

mint—the making of coins; also, the place where coins are made.

money supply—the amount of money in the economy

nondurable goods—goods that are routinely used by consumers, such as food and clothing

principal—the amount of money borrowed or loaned, not counting interest

silver-backed—money that can be exchanged for an equal amount of silver upon request

specie—coin money

stock—partial ownership in a business

store of value—the capability of money to hold its purchasing power over time

Treasury bond—a loan of money to government

INDEX

ACKNOWLEDGMENTS

The photographs and illustrations in this book are used courtesy of: Department of the Treasury/Bureau of Engraving and Printing, pp. 1, 22; LeeAnne Engfer, pp. 6, 15, 24, 26, 31, 34, 36, 56, 71, 75, 82, 85, 89; Israel Museum, Department of Antiquities and Museums, Ministry of Culture, Israel, p. 9; the Bodleian Library, Oxford/Ms. Bodley 764, 13th-century bestiary, ff.44, p. 10; Cambridge University Library/Ms. Ee. 3.59, f4r, p. 12; Federal Reserve Bank of Minneapolis, pp. 17, 23, 59, 73; St. Paul Postal Employees Credit Union, p. 32; the Mansell Collection, p. 39; Library of Congress, pp. 42, 43; Independent Picture Service, p. 45; Minnesota Historical Society, p. 46; Norwest Corporation, p. 51; Norwest Bank Owatonna, p. 53; Audio Visual Resource Department, Maine Medical Center, p. 54; Ford Motor Company Limited, p. 62; Federal Reserve Bank of New York, p. 64; Minnesota Department of Transportation, p. 66; Richard Trombley, p. 86; National Archives, p. 96.

The charts and illustrations on pages 21, 28, 69, and 78 are by Bryan Liedahl.

Front cover photograph courtesy of LeeAnne Engfer. Back cover photograph courtesy of the Federal Reserve Bank of Minneapolis.